SURVIVING

AMERICAN

HISTORY

MAX HOWARD

An imprint of Enslow Publishing

WEST **44** BOOKS™

Please visit our website, www.west44books.com.
For a free color catalog of all our high-quality books,
call toll free 1-800-398-2504.

Cataloging-in-Publication Data

Names: Howard, Max.
Title: Surviving American history / Max Howard.
Description: New York : West 44, 2022.
Identifiers: ISBN 9781978595484 (pbk.) | ISBN 9781978595644
(library bound) | ISBN 9781978595507 (ebook)
Subjects: LCSH: Poetry, American--21st century. | English poetry. |
Young adult poetry, American. | Poetry, Modern--21st century.
Classification: LCC PS586.3 S875 2022 | DDC 811'.60809282--dc23

First Edition

Published in 2022 by
Enslow Publishing LLC
29 East 21st Street
New York, NY 10010

Editor: Caitie McAneney
Designer: Tanya Dellaccio
Interior Layout: Rachel Rising

Photo Credits: Cover, pp. 1-187 design36/Shutterstock.com.

Printed in the United States of America

CPSIA compliance information: Batch #CS22W44: For further information contact
Enslow Publishing LLC, New York, New York at 1-800-398-2504.

GOODBYE, GODEY HIGH

The halls are
empty. Everyone's in
class. Mom's
waiting for me
outside in the
U-Haul truck.

Goodbye,
STRIVE FOR EXCELLENCE
banner.

Adios, Growth
Mindset poster.

Farewell, 10
a.m. aroma of
fresh French fries.

Goodbye.
Namaste.

NAMASTE

It's third period.
Ava's in Broadcast Media.
She wants to be a radio reporter.
I'm *supposed* to be in
American history.

Instead I'm
moving to Maine.

I open Ava's locker.
Put on her lemon lotion.
Now I smell like Ava.

I take a last
look at her
locker. It's
super tidy.
Except for the
mirror.

She's lipsticked
the word
Namaste
on the glass.

THE GLASS

Behind the
lipsticked letters
I see my face.
It's a mess
from crying.

Namaste.
Ava and I
learned the word
two years ago,
during our first
yoga class.
It means:
*The light in me
bows to the light in you.*

Now I don't
just study
yoga. I'm a
certified
teacher, too.

At the end of
my teen yoga class,
we all say
Namaste.

It's a good way to end things.

A GOOD WAY TO END THINGS

Leaving, I pass
Ms. Lin's room.
American history.
I'm supposed
to be in there. But I
stand outside, listening.

Ms. Lin is Ava's mom. Her
home voice is fluttery. Her
school voice is firm.

She's talking about the
Civil War: guns and
dead bodies.

"Some of the
soldiers were
your age,"
she says, her
firm voice cracking.

CRACKING

I saw part of a
Civil War video
last week. Ms. Lin
previewed it at
home while she
cracked eggs into
brownie mix.

"This video is
only showing
dead white kids.
What about Black soldiers
who fought?" Ava said.
"Wasn't slavery what the
war was all about?"
She stuck her finger in the
batter, licked.

"Ava, you have a point.
But next time, use a
spoon," Ms. Lin
scolded. She poured
batter into a pan.
"Gabi. You're the guest.
Would you like to
lick the bowl?"

THE BOWL

Mom turns
into the
strip mall parking lot,
passes Friendly Fro-Yo,
passes Godey Gun Shop,
parks in front of
Bliss Yoga.

"OK, honey.
Take a last
look while I
text Jason."

That's her
new boyfriend.
He's hypnotized her.
That's why
we're moving.

Mom set Jason's
text tone to Meditation
Bowl. I hate the
sound. The
bowl tone
wrecked my life.

I look at my old studio.

MY OLD STUDIO

Long yellow curtains
glow in the
glass doors.

When I own
my own studio,
I'll have yellow
curtains too.

Who knows
what kind of
curtains
they have in
Maine? There's
a studio in our
new town, but the
website is just a
picture of the
stupid ocean.

I take a deep breath.
Count to four.
Exhale six
counts of hot
CO_2.
It's calming.

No matter where I go,
I take my breath with me.
That's yoga.

THAT'S YOGA

Ava and I wore the
same size
until sixth grade.
Then my body
started turning into
my mom's body:
short and round.

At first, I
crashed into walls,
not knowing my
new size. I wanted to
look like my dad's
mom from Mexico,
who is slim and small.
Instead I looked like a
German dumpling:
fluffy, chubby, thick.

Words
circling a
stigma.
I didn't feel
fat. I felt
shame.

And then
I walked
through those
yellow curtains.

YELLOW CURTAINS

Walk through the yellow
curtains and into Bliss
Yoga.

Smell oranges.
Hear chimes.

See people
posing like
animals.

Old people
doing puppy
pose. Young
people doing
cat-cow. Fat
people doing
crow. Skinny
people doing
frog.

At the end, everyone
lies down. Basks like
lions in the sun.

LIONS IN THE SUN

Yoga helps me
learn to love
my animal
body.

I'm learning to love
my human
heart, too.

I'm learning
to be the
basking
lion and the
shining sun.

THE SHINING SUN

Cornfields
flash by at
55 miles per hour. The
sunlit husks
gleam, gold and
dead.

We're moving to
Maine, leaving
Dad behind, and
Ava, and everyone—
all because of
Mom's high school
boyfriend.

MOM'S HIGH SCHOOL BOYFRIEND

Ava does a great
radio reporter voice.
We used to sit in the cafeteria
and she did the news,
like:

Breaking: Kaleb Kostyak
has just rubbed
Cheeto powder
all over his pants.

Or: *A new study shows that*
70% of teachers
fart backward.

Or: *Headline News:*
Woman, 45, finds
love on Facebook,
ruins family.

I already miss Ava.
I look at Mom. She
snaps her gum.
Gross. I breathe
slowly, trying to
quiet my mind, when
both our phones
start blowing up.

BLOWING UP

It's Dad.
I answer.
He says,
"Thank God"
then cuts out.

"I only have
two bars
out here," I say.
The call
drops.

Mom's phone
rings.
She yells
"What? WHAT?"
into her phone.

Then she looks
away from the
road, messing with
the radio. Our truck
veers toward the
ditch.

OUR TRUCK VEERS TOWARD THE DITCH

I grab the wheel,
straighten us out.
Mom barely blinks.
Her face looks
frozen.

Then I hear it.
Ava's news reporter voice.
It crackles through the
truck's radio.

This is WQRW,
Godey High Radio.
We are live.
We are alive.
But we're hearing gunshots.

WE'RE HEARING GUNSHOTS

At *first we thought*
they were fireworks,
Ava says.

Her voice is steady
but someone is
crying in the
background.

She sounds calm.
She'll make a good reporter,
I think. Then
fear slices
through my chest.

She'll make a good reporter—
if she makes it out alive.

ALIVE.

When I hear
Ava's
voice, her
breath, I know
she's alive.
Keep talking,
I pray.

But we're 30
miles from Godey High.

Ava's voice
cuts in
and
out
then

static
blasts us.

Is she okay?
Is she alive?

ALIVE?

"There's a hill
about a mile
away," Mom says,
"we can get
better reception
at the top."

She floors it.
The truck
lurches. Her
blond ponytail
flies back.
At 90 miles per hour,
the truck groans and
shakes. I
turn up
the radio.
Static hisses.
Please,
please be alive!

ALIVE!

Mom pulls over
at the top of the
hill. I twist the
radio dial.

And there she is—
Ava!

Her voice is
calm.
Like a reporter's.

I repeat, we have an
active shooter.

A bell rings.

I shudder.
I know that sound.
"That's fourth period,"
I say. "Fourth period
is starting."

FOURTH PERIOD IS STARTING

But no one
at Godey is
changing
classes. I can
picture it.
I know the
lockdown
drills. I've
hidden
behind the
teacher's desk,
my arm
pressed
against
hunky Hunter
Jackson's,
wondering
if this time
it was real.

THIS TIME IT WAS REAL

Ava's voice is
faint.

She says she loves her
family. She says she
loves her
best friend,
Gabi.

That's me.

THAT'S ME

That's me, holding my
breath. Drowning
every time
static swallows
Ava's voice.

At last
she says,

*The police are
here. We're safe.
But we don't know
if others are hurt.*

Her voice cracks.
*This is WQRW.
We're broadcasting from
Godey High,
where we
Strive for Excellence.
I'm Ava Lin,
signing off.*

I can breathe again.
Mom cranks the wheel.
We roar out of Iowa.

#IOWA

As soon as I get
signal, I text Ava.
I wait.

Check the hashtags
#Iowa and #IowaShooting
on Twitter.

"At least 15
are dead," I say.
"Turn around.
We have to go home."

Mom shakes
her head, says,
"We can't.
I have to be
at my new job
Monday."

We pass a sign.
Welcome to Illinois.

Ava texts back.
We're in the football field.
Everybody is lining up.
I can't find my mom.

I unbuckle my
seat belt,
slide next to
Mom. She smells like
face powder.

I text Ava.
I bet she's helping with
        everything.

But I know it's
not true. If Ms. Lin were
okay, she'd be
comforting Ava.

I hold
onto my
mom all the
way to
Ohio.

OHIO

Starbucks
after
Starbucks.
Text after
text. Tweet
after
tweet.

Who's alive?
Who's dead?
Who did it?
There are
rumors. But
no one knows.

NO ONE KNOWS

I'm learning new
words.

Red tag
yellow tag
black tag

My friend Shayla
got shot in the
hall. She's
okay. Tweeting
now. Telling how
she lay there
bleeding. Hearing
everything. Shots.
Screams.

The police came and
sorted everyone out.

Yellow tag - can wait, will live.
Red tag - hurry, might die.
Black tag - dead.

Shayla got a
Yellow Tag.

YELLOW TAG

Hotel orange
juice. Pale,
sour. Dry
breakfast buffet
muffins. CNN on
TVs everywhere.
Strangers
chew cereal and
watch. A reporter
stands in front of my school.
Her hair is perfect.
Twenty-six people are dead.

In the hotel
dining room,
a woman with
donut sugar
on her face says,
"Tragedy."

TRAGEDY

"Eat a bite of
cereal," Mom
says.

I sweep my arm
across the
table.

My
paper hotel
cereal bowl
goes flying.

Milk splatters
on the TV.

Drips
down the
newscaster's
perfect hair.

"Take me home,"
I tell Mom.
"We have to
go back.
I don't even know who's
alive, who's dead."

DEAD

My friends
hid under
desks, hearing
gunshots.

I hide my eyes
listening to
the radio.

Our truck
roars down the
highway.

We cross into
New York.

This is NPR and a
woman is saying the
names of the dead.

THE NAMES OF THE DEAD

This list is
familiar.

I've heard it
before.

I heard it
every day
during
roll call.

ROLL CALL

Shayla lay
bleeding in the hall
outside of
American history
hearing
black tag
      black tag
            black tag

                              black tag
black tag black tag

                          black tag
 black tag
black tag
     black tag

          black tag
black tag

black tag   *black tag*

black tag
     black tag
                   black tag
   black tag black tag
            black tag

black tag black tag black tag

black tag
     black tag   *black tag*

30

BLACK TAG

Everyone from
Ms. Lin's
third period
American
history class is
dead.

Everyone except
"one student,
who was absent."
Me.

Emma Juvenal, who
sat next to me is
dead. Jesse Bly is
dead. So is
Kaitlyn Robertson, the
tiny girl who played the
tuba.

Even Ms. Lin.
Ava's mom.

AVA'S MOM

Ava's Mom is
dead. Kaleb Kostyak is
dead. That is, no
longer eating
Cheetos and
wiping them on his
pants. Alex
Kruger won't
skate past my
house ever again.
Because he's dead.
They're all dead,
all 26 of them.
Connor Alvarez to
Paige Zabawski.
Everyone from
American history
is dead.

Except me.

EXCEPT ME

The Atlantic Ocean
hisses, washing over
my feet.

"It's too cold
to wade,"
Mom yells.
She sits on
the hood of the car,
texting Jason.
"March is still winter in
Maine."

The waves
rush in. As they
pull back, the sand
slips from
beneath my
numb feet.

Not even the earth
is steady.

STEADY

I spend all
day on the couch
in our rented
house. I can't
find blankets.
So I pile on
towels.

Shayla texts.

Ava doesn't.

Shayla texts again.

Get on Twitter.
They're saying
who did it.
Hunter Jackson.

HUNTER JACKSON

The media
posts pics
from Hunter's
profile.

In a Halloween photo,
Hunter has his
arm around me.
He's a pirate.
I'm a butterfly.

I've looked at this
picture many times,
wondering if
Hunter liked me.

Now strangers
comment about the
shooter's
fat girlfriend.

I don't believe it.
How could
Hunter be the
shooter? He doesn't even
play paintball.

PAINTBALL

Six people in my
text thread tell about
creepy stuff
Hunter has done:
like giving them
weird looks. Or
drawing devils in
art. Or making
dead baby jokes.

Then the truth
comes out.
The media
got mixed up.
Everyone else did,
too.

Hunter Jackson
isn't the shooter.
Jackson Hunter is.

JACKSON HUNTER

No one
really knows
Jackson.

He's a senior.
He *was* a senior—
until one day he
got up, ate a
strawberry
Pop Tart, and
killed 25 people and
himself.

He bought his
guns two weeks ago at
Godey Gun Shop.
The place next to
Bliss Yoga.

Was I there, at
Bliss, when he
bought guns to
kill us all? Was I
bowing, saying
Namaste?
Believing in a
light that lives in
everyone?

EVERYONE

"It's been
three weeks.
Experts say
you need to
get off
social media.
Start a routine,"
Mom says. "I'm
putting you in
school."

"But I want to go home."
My voice is
choppy. Like
I've been running.
It's weird.
Sometimes I can't
catch my breath.

I want to go home.
Hug Ava and
Dad. Sign
Shayla's cast.
Light candles.
Cry with everyone.

But Mom
won't listen.

MOM WON'T LISTEN

I call Dad,
beg him to
buy me a plane
ticket.

"What does your mom say?"

"She wants me to
start school."

"Then you
should," he says.
"I'm too
tired to argue with her."

I tell him this
lazy behavior is
exactly why
Mom left him.

Which is true.
Mean.
But true.
I think.

THINK

My new school
is on a little
island.

We drive across
a narrow bridge
to get there.

The principal
shows me
the counselor's office.

Says I can go
there anytime.
But I'm thinking
about the bridge.

THE BRIDGE

There's only
one way off
the island:
the bridge.

A shooter could just
wait for the final
bell. Then
block the bridge.
Kill us all
on our way home.

If that
happens, I'll
jump off. I'd
rather die
in the ocean.

THE OCEAN

Even in school, I can hear the waves.

No one else seems to notice them.

The sea sobs.

(Whiteboard markers squeak away.)

The ocean grinds its teeth.

(Kids eat Frito pie in the smelly cafeteria.)

The sea hurls itself against rocks.

My chest aches from
holding my
breath. I
can't let it
go.
Even the
sound of
my own
exhale
hurts.

Mom tells me to adjust.

ADJUST

I'm late to
class because
I'm watching
people in the hallway.

Everyone is
so beautiful.
So temporary.

I watch
hands. When
people
talk, their hands
turn into
butterflies.

Fingers are
amazing, too.
They twist in hair,
spin combination
locks, unwrap
gum, scratch
noses.

I can't help
but stare.

No wonder everyone
thinks I'm weird.

WEIRD

Even Haley Kaye
is beautiful
to me.

She's the kind of girl
boys love:
sticky with
makeup and
mean.

"Do you like my
lip gloss?" she
asks me.

I nod.

She swoops in,
kisses me
hard on the
mouth.

Her lip gloss
tastes like
coconut.

She sneers:
"I don't care if you're a
lesbian. Just try not to
stare so much."

STARE SO MUCH

The principal
snaps her
fingers.

"Haley! A word, please."

Haley licks her
coconut lips.
Then she goes to the
office.

When she comes back,
things change.

People don't stare at me
like I'm the new girl.

They stare at me
like I'm a ghost.

I'M A GHOST

Mr. Burgos is
so old. He looks
like he's made
of dust. He hands out
Moby Dick.

"Spoiler alert,"
he says.
"There's a shipwreck
in this book."

Outside, the ocean
thrashes. Mr. Burgos
keeps talking:

"Not everyone goes
down with the ship.
Someone has to live to tell
the tale. Turn
to the last page.
Melville
puts it this way:
'And I only am escaped alone
to tell thee.'"

ALONE TO TELL THEE

Ava won't
text me back.

But I see her
on TV.

I hear her
reporter voice
on the radio.

The media
found her
WQRW broadcast.

Now she's invited
on talk shows.
She gets thousands of
retweets.

(She tweets a lot.
But never at me.)

Newscasters love her.
They're calling her a
hero and the
future of journalism.

THE FUTURE OF JOURNALISM

I know
Ava's not a hero.
She's just a girl
who misses her mom.

Maybe that's why
she won't text me back.
She wants to be a hero.
Not a girl who hurts.

A GIRL WHO HURTS

I video chat
Shayla. It's good
to see her face, her
smile—everything has
changed but she's still
wearing hot coral
lipstick, bright
against her dark brown
skin. She
brings me to a
wake, carries me
around on her
phone. Like
I'm her
candle.

Now she yells,
"I've got Gabi on
my phone!"
People swarm. My screen
crowds with
faces. Voices.
We love you, Gabi!
We miss you.

WE MISS YOU

Mom: "We miss you.
That's why
I'm taking your phone."

Me: "Who's we?"

Mom: "Jason and I."

Me: "Jason? Your boyfriend?
He doesn't even know me."

Mom: "Let him get to know you."

Me: "You can't take my phone.
Ava might call."

Mom: "Let's try it for one night.
It's just dinner."

IT'S JUST DINNER

At the restaurant, Jason
butters me up with
lobster.

I can't
swallow. Or
hate him. Or feel
anything.

Someone's left a
newspaper on a
table. Ms. Lin
smiles on the
front page.

A busboy
puts the
paper in a
dirty tub full of lobster
claws.

CLAWS

A month
after it happened,
I take my first
yoga class.

Go Go Yoga is
nothing like
Bliss.

Go Go has
bright lights,
huge mirrors and
yelling:

faster
harder
stronger
hotter
fitter
thinner

Also.

Haley's in this class, too.

HALEY'S IN THIS CLASS, TOO

During
tree pose,
Haley eyes me
up and
down
in the mirror.

Her gaze
zooms in
on my round
belly.

I try
to focus
on a spot
on the floor.
(That's how you keep
your balance.)
But I can feel
my breath
building up
in my chest.

Haley
looks at me,
and I
wobble.

WOBBLE

The thing is,
Haley looks like
Paige Zabawski
from American
history class.

Paige used to
make my
skin sting with
shame. She was so
pretty.

Shayla has a theory.
She's not sure.
But she thinks
Paige and Jackson
were secretly
dating. Then Paige
dumped Jackson.
So he killed her, and
everyone. Who knows
if it's true?

Still.

Why would
anyone want to be
beautiful?
Why do I?

I fall out of tree pose.

FALL OUT OF TREE POSE

After class,
I zip my jacket and
head outside.
Bye-bye,
Go Go Yoga.
I take a shortcut home.
Cut through a
gap in a holly hedge.
My foot catches
on something. I crash
through the holly and
fall on a boy and
his bike. "Sorry,
I didn't see you," I say,
but I'm
seeing him
now.

I'M SEEING HIM NOW

A guy with laughing eyes,
freckles, and dark hair
sticking up
just the right way.

Suddenly I feel
something wild—
it's like a bird
got trapped
inside my chest.

I turn and
run,
scared.

*What's happening
in my chest?
Am I dying?*
I wonder. Then I
get it.

*This is a
feeling and
I am alive.*

THIS IS A FEELING AND I AM ALIVE

At school,
I see Holly Boy.
He's leaning up against
Haley's locker.

He's holding
her hand with his
eyes closed.
He's wearing big
headphones.

The bird flops around
in my chest.

The bird has no right
to be in there,
trying to live
when everyone
is dead.

WHEN EVERYONE IS DEAD

I'm doing
yoga on the
freezing beach.
Where else
can I be alone?

Moving my body
used to calm me.

But now
my mind takes me
back to
American history.

The waves bring me
sounds: Kaleb clicking
his pen. Connor
taking forever at
the pencil sharpener.
Paige's squeaky
sneeze.

I put my
hands up,
cover my
ears, and scream.

SCREAM

"Hey!" someone yells.
I turn around.

It's Holly Boy.

He's standing
way above me
on a boulder.

Black jeans,
black hoodie.
Thumbs sticking
out from
holes in his
sleeves.

He leans down.
Offers me his
headphones.
"Maybe these will
help."

HELP

Holly Boy
lets the
headphones
drop.

I catch them,
slip them
over my ears.

I'm expecting
music.

Instead, I hear
silence.

Even the ocean
shuts up.

EVEN THE OCEAN SHUTS UP

When I
open my eyes,
he's gone.

I climb
up on the
rocks.

When I reach
the top of
the boulder,
I see him.

He's already
        far away.

With his
hood up,
he looks like a
comma.

I put his
headphones on.
The silence feels
like a hug.

HUG

I wake up
from a
nightmare.

My room is
dark. Mom's
snoring.

But I'm still hearing
gunshots
from my dream:

BANG!
BANG!
BANG!

Last time,
Mom told me
the noise was
just the radiator.

So I slip the
headphones
on. Fall
asleep, safe
in their quiet.

QUIET

Everyone stops
talking when I
walk up to
Haley's table
in the cafeteria.

(I don't care.
I'm just glad
everyone's alive.)

I drop the
headphones
on the table.
Slide them
to Holly Boy.

Haley's eyes
narrow. She's
mad. It's
almost cute.

I walk away.
Haley says,

"Lennon?
Why did she have
your headphones?
Lennon?"

LENNON

So now I know his name.
Thanks, Haley.

Lennon.

I hold the
name in my
mind. It's hard to
stop your
worst thoughts.

But a
mantra,
a word you
think
instead of your
thoughts,
helps.

Saying a mantra
is like pushing
desks in front of the
door during
lockdown.
It keeps you
busy, so you
don't feel afraid.

Lennon.

Again, I feel the bird
in my chest.

THE BIRD IN MY CHEST

The bird in my chest
squeaks
when I close
my locker and
see Lennon's
face.

"Let's ditch
sixth," he says.

I shake
my head no.

He says,
"Why not?
Life is short."

Then he walks
away, a
fast, dark comma.
I run to keep up.

KEEP UP

Lennon bikes us
into town. I ride on
the handlebars.
They bite
into my thighs.

Maybe the handlebars
wouldn't
dig in so much if I
weren't so heavy,
if I looked
more like
Haley.

The ocean wind
blasts the
shame from my mind.

We cross the bridge.

The bird
inside my chest
dives into the
wild breeze and
soars.

It's a
good feeling.

GOOD FEELING

"Downtown is
so cute," I say.
The brick
buildings are old
but tidy. Toy
lobsters and
sailboats
fill shop windows.
Lennon shrugs.
"It's all for tourists."

He ditches his
bike in some
bushes, then
leads me
into an alley.
Says, "Let's
hide."

We squeeze behind
some trash cans.
His arm feels
warm against
mine. I don't
look like Haley.
But maybe—
maybe?

MAYBE

A man wearing an
apron steps into the
alley. He throws a black
trash bag into the
dumpster.

When he leaves,
Lennon opens the
dumpster.
He dares me:

"Put your hand
inside the
trash bag."

I'm scared of
rats. But I do it.

I feel something
soft. Almost
furry.

I jump back.

Lennon laughs.
He opens the bag.
It's full of
powdered
sugar donuts.

DONUTS

Lennon throws the bag
over his shoulder.
We walk through the town.
"You look like Santa," I say.

He says,
"Ho, Ho, Ho!"
Then he stuffs a
jelly donut in the
mail slot
of the door of an
insurance office.

"Donut delivery!"
he shouts,
pounding on the door.
We run away.
Running feels
just like laughing.

LAUGHING

We walk and
eat donuts.
At the edge of town,
there's a graveyard.
It's old.
Maine old.
Some of the
graves are from the
1700s.

Many of the gravestones
are tiny. They're
for babies. Kids
who died 300 years ago.

We put donuts
on the kids' graves.
I ask,
"Why are you
hanging out with me?
Do you feel sorry for me?"

SORRY FOR ME

"No," he says. "I thought
maybe you'd understand me.
No one else does."

Seagulls loop
through the air,
screaming and
bleating. They
zoom in, pluck
donuts off the graves.

"Look out," Lennon says.
"Seagulls will poop on you and steal your
food."

FOOD

When I get home,
the kitchen smells like steak.
Jason sits at the
table, chewing.

"The school called,"
Mom says.
"You skipped.
That's a major
breach of trust."

I laugh.

"Trust," I say.

Trust?

TRUST

"Trust? Like how
Dad *trusted* you
not to cheat?"
I say.

Mom's face
goes white.
She says,
"Gabi, stop. We're
not talking about
me right now.
We're talking about
you."

WE'RE TALKING ABOUT YOU

"This is about
me?" I say.
"When has anything
ever been about me?
My friends got
murdered. You
didn't even
take me to their
funerals.
Why? Because
you wanted to
hang out
with your boyfriend."

"Gabi, please,"
Mom says.
"I'm trying to
help you get
back to normal.
Put this behind you.
It's for your own
good."

"No," I say. "It's for *your* own good.
 Like everything you do."

EVERYTHING YOU DO

I run to my room, and
text Ava. Shayla.
Dad.

I listen to Mom
telling Jason
she's *sorry about Gabi's
behavior.*

Shayla sends me
an angry bitmoji.
Dad sends me
a *That's too bad,
kiddo.* Such
weak sauce.

Ava says
nothing.
Why would she?
I'm complaining
about my mom—
when hers is
dead.

In the kitchen,
Jason says,
"I get it. Gabi's
going through a lot."

GOING THROUGH A LOT

When I walk by
Haley's locker,
she grabs Lennon.
Kisses him.

I smile.
Who cares?

Haley doesn't
understand him.
I do.

I DO

Yesterday Lennon
told me about
his twin sister,
Lily. He
showed me her
grave. She
overdosed.
Lennon found her.
His family thinks
it was as an
accident. He
thinks it was
suicide. "She used
all her drugs," he
said. "She wanted
to die." A seagull
screamed. Lennon
covered his ears.
He said, "Since she died,
sounds are too loud."
He touched the
headphones around
his neck. "These help.
They put you in a
cozy tomb."

A COZY TOMB

We're starting the
Civil War unit in
American history.

The teacher shows us
the exact same video
Ms. Lin showed us:
old photographs of dead
young white people. Fiddle
music. Cannon
sound effects.

I think of Ava
sticking her
finger in the
batter, complaining
about this video.

I text her,
The Civil War again.

THE CIVIL WAR AGAIN

I wait.
Ava doesn't text back.
Are the two of us in a
civil war? Does she
even read my texts?

I send them anyway.
She loves to fight
about ideas.
So I try out a few.

It's the Civil War
all over again.
Adults in government
keep fighting.
Meanwhile bodies
pile up.
Mostly kids.

I stare at my phone for a long time.
Shayla says it's
not just me.
Ava is pushing
everyone away.

PUSHING EVERYONE AWAY

No one
really knows
why Jackson Hunter
shot everyone.

But the
media found pictures of
his truck. Ava goes on
TV to talk about it.

Her hair is perfect.
She says,

This class was
studying the Civil War.
They were all
killed by a
kid with a
Confederate
flag bumper sticker.
Don't you see
what's happening?

Face it,
Ava says.
This is the
Civil War, Part Two.
This time the issue
isn't slavery. It's
power. Adults
in Washington argue
while kids' bodies
pile up. We're dying
from guns. But
also from
poverty. Inequality.
Of course,
racism. We
should have fixed that
after the first time
we went to war.
We didn't.
Now it's on us.

Ava's using my words.
It means she's
reading my texts
even if she doesn't
text back.

SHE DOESN'T TEXT BACK

But she retweets the
death threats
she's getting online.

Some people
don't like
what she has
to say. Some
don't like
that she's
Chinese-American.
Others say,
Shut up.
Let the adults do
the talking.

"Gabi?" Mr. Burgos
says. He holds out his
dusty old hand.
"No phones in class."

NO PHONES IN CLASS

My phone is
how I check
to see
who is still
alive.

Mr. Burgos
puts it in
his desk.

My chest feels
tight. Like
someone's
squeezing the
breath out
of it.

Mr. Burgos
turns to write
on the board.

"I need some air,"
I mutter, then
get up and
walk out.

WALK OUT

Yesterday
Mom gave me a
journal. It
says *#Gratitude*
on the cover.

She thought
I'd like it.
Gratitude is
big in yoga.

I said,
"What am I
supposed to write?
I'm glad
everyone else
died, not me?"

I see
Lennon at
at his locker.

Hmm.

#Gratitude

#GRATITUDE

I grab Lennon's hand
and start running.

We burst
through the door
into the cool
spring air.

Lennon doesn't
ask where
we're going.
Just bikes me
into town.

The sky is gray.
The sea breeze
blows my hair.
It makes the
daffodils fly too.

THE DAFFODILS

Lennon
pedals.
I balance on the
handlebars.
We yell over
the wind.

"Everything
happens for
a reason. Ever
hear that one?"
Lennon shouts.

I snort.
"Really?
Kids get murdered
for a good reason?
That kind of
inspo junk is why
I can't even
do yoga videos
anymore."

Lennon says,
"Yep. It's all
empty promises."

EMPTY PROMISES

Lennon's parents have a
sailboat. It's stored in
a warehouse. Lennon says,

"They'll bring the
boat out Memorial
Day weekend.
Put the mast up.
My parents will
come home for a
month and sail it.
Then they'll leave
again."

The warehouse is full of
huge, gleaming
boats.

"Shh," Lennon says.
"They're sleeping."

SLEEPING

We climb into
Lennon's parents'
boat. The cabin
is the best
part. A booth
with a table
turns into
a bed. Couches
store blankets.

I lie down on
a leather couch.
Lennon lies down
on the floor
next to me.

He reaches up,
tugs at
my shoelaces.
Says,

"So what happened
today?"

Where do I
begin? My
phone in Mr. Burgos's
desk? My breath
catching? The
gun shop in the
strip mall, next to
my old yoga studio?
Ava's voice
crackling
through the
radio? Ms.
Lin in her
snowman pajamas
when I'd sleep
over at Ava's?
The wake
Shayla took me to
on a video-chat app?
I open my
mouth and say,

SAY

"My best friend
won't talk
to me
anymore."

My voice
sounds
choked.

Lennon
squeezes
my toes
through
my sneakers.

"I feel like
a jerk. Some
people lost
their best
friends. I'm
just lonely."

LONELY

"It's okay,"
Lennon says.
"However you feel.
It's okay."

I say,
"My mom wants
me to get
over it. Put it
behind me."

"That's idiotic,"
Lennon says.

He squeezes
my ankle.
His hand
makes my
whole body
feel warm.

I kick
him away,
saying,

"I wasn't supposed to live."

"Me neither,"
Lennon says.
"I had cancer
when I was a
kid. Lily,
my sister,
saved my
life. They
took her
bone marrow.
Transplanted
it into
me. I
lived.
So did she.
Lily was smarter
than me.
Funnier.
Nicer.
I don't
get it.
Why am I
here, and she's
not? Why
me?"

WHY ME?

I let my hand
fall so my
fingers
brush the
floor near
his hair.
I pluck
a dark
silky
strand,
wind it around
my finger.

"You have
good hair,"
I say.
"Maybe that's
why
you survived."

"You have good hair
too," Lennon says.
"That's probably
why we're
both alive."

I start to
laugh, but
Lennon
jumps up and
covers
my mouth.

"The guard,"
he whispers.

We can hear
someone walking
between the boats.

We hold
still. The
giggles build
inside me
until I'm shaking.

"Hello?" The guard
calls. "Hello?"

HELLO

Hello, welcome to the Civil War 2.0 Podcast, Ava says.

Her reporter voice sounds great.
Her first weekly podcast gets 10,000 downloads.

She interviews kids from school.
Also, the governor.

But then Ava's podcast starts coming out daily. Not weekly.
The podcasts are hours long. She reads news articles from the Civil War.
She reads tweets from dead kids.
She talks herself hoarse.

I listen.

Lennon lives with
his grandma, Mrs. Wood.
She's so old,
her hands
shake when she
pours tea.

Her house
is old, too—almost
as old as the graveyard.
There's a widow's walk
on the roof.

Mrs. Wood says,
"My great-grandfather
was lost at sea.
This was his house.
His wife
walked the roof
every day
looking for his
ship until she died.
Cream and sugar?"

CREAM AND SUGAR

Mrs. Wood's
teacups are from
before the
Civil War.
I'm afraid
to hold one,
but she
passes it to me
anyway. It's
tiny and
painted with roses.

"I think the three of us are
all waiting for people.
Aren't we?" Mrs. Wood
pats my hand. "Are you two
planning to go back to
school today,
or not?"

OR NOT

Lennon has the whole
attic to himself.

We lie on his bed,
listening to the roof
creak.

"That's the widow's ghost
walking the roof,"
Lennon says.

He leans close.
Puts headphones over my ears.
All sound vanishes.

I close my eyes.

When his lips
meet mine,
everything that
ever happened
vanishes.

Later, I say,
"Are you still going out with Haley? Or
not."

"Not," he says.
"Not exactly."

EXACTLY

I tell Lennon,
"My dad called.
He said my
mom told him
to tell me
to stop
skipping school.
If I do,
he'll buy me
a plane ticket
home for a visit."

We laugh.
"That stuff used to
work on me.
The carrot.
The stick.
If you're good,
something good will
happen. But
now I know life is
random,"
Lennon says.
"Might as well
do what you want."

DO WHAT YOU WANT

One night,
Lennon and I
climb up
the fire escape
on the side of
the bank building.

We take a selfie
on the roof.
It's a full moon.
The whole
town looks
black and white.

So do we.

It's like
living in a
1950s movie.

Lennon grabs my phone.
Sends the selfie to
himself and to Ava.

"You're crazy,"
I say. He says,

"I want to talk to her.
You're the best
friend ever.
I see what she
can't see."

100

CAN'T SEE

It's easy to
jump from the
bank roof
to the building
next door, then
climb in
an open window.

I find myself in
the balcony of
Captain Crab's Grill.
The place where
Jason bribed me
with lobster.

It's so dark.
"I can't see,"
I say, laughing,
crashing down stairs,
knocking into tables.

Lennon finds a
vodka bottle.
We twirl on the
barstools in the
dark.

THE DARK

The vodka
burns my throat.
It makes my
stomach hurt.
"Haley would
never do this,"
Lennon says.
"She cares
too much about
swim team." He
passes me the bottle.

I take a sip
because Haley
wouldn't.

My phone
rings.
It's Ava.
Ava!
She's calling me.

But before
I can answer it,
Lennon kisses
me.

I let
Ava go
to voicemail.

VOICEMAIL

I listen to
Ava's message.
It's strange.
I don't hear *her* voice.
I hear her
radio reporter voice.

*I'm sorry I missed
your calls. It's been busy.
CNN offered me a
summer internship.
I'm up for a Youth in
Media Prize. And
I'm speaking at a
conference. In Boston.
That's not too far
from Maine. If I have
time, maybe I'll
come see you over
Memorial Day. It's
not for sure. I might
be too busy.*

BUSY

Mom said she was
"busy"
working late.
(Really she
was cheating on
Dad.)

Dad was always
"busy"–napping
with a newspaper
over his face.

(Really
he was just
pretending
not to know
what Mom was
up to.)

Being busy
is just a way
to lie to yourself.

LIE TO YOURSELF

After school,
I go to Lennon's.
We listen to
records in his
room.

"Ava's coming to
visit," I say. "Over
Memorial Day."

He grins.
"Really? That's
so great. We can
take her sailing."

We kiss.
His lips
feel sticky.
They taste like
coconut.

COCONUT

"What's the matter?"
Lennon asks.

"You taste like Haley,"
I say.

He shrugs. Says,
"She can remember Lily."

REMEMBER LILY

"Seriously?" I say.
"You kissed Haley?"

Lennon says,
"I thought you
understood.
Death is
freedom. It
shows you
all the
petty little rules are
stupid."

"Right," I say.
"Because it's not
cheating if you have
a dead sister!"

I run out of the house
so fast I don't even say
goodbye to
Mrs. Wood.

MRS. WOOD

The temp hits
60. Mom
makes me
get an ice cream cone
with her.

Walking home,
we see Mrs. Wood.

Her paper
shopping bag splits.
Cans of soup
roll over the sidewalk.

Mom and I
run to help her.
Mrs. Wood pats my
arm with her
shaky hand, says,
"Thanks, Gabi."

Mom asks,
"How do you know her?"

The question hurts.

HURTS

In chemistry, we
read about
moss. Civil War
people used it
as a bandage.
Scientists
say it
actually works.
Something about
ions. Lennon
raises his
hand and
answers a
question.

His voice tears
a scab from
my heart.

I'm losing
blood.
I hold
my breath.
Try not to
fall
apart in
chemistry.

CHEMISTRY

Mom loves talking on the phone.
She tells her
Iowa friends how
happy she is. She wants
everyone to leave their
husband. "Pull off the
Band-Aid," she says.
"Go for it."

I snort. Jason is just as
dull as my dad.
Plus he has
half as much hair.

Mom gushes, "The chemistry is insane."

INSANE

Shayla and I
video chat.
She says,
"It's weird. No one
is who they used to be.
Ava won't talk
to anyone. She's
saving her voice.
Hunter Jackson
quit football.
The mathletes have gone
ape. They refuse to go to
school at all. Instead
they sit outside
the town hall,
protesting."

Even Shayla,
the dancer and
drama queen,
is different. She
says she's clumsy.
Always running into things.
Crashing.

CRASHING

The principal needs to
cut her nails. They're
long and
wavy. Like a witch's.

"Gabi, do you think
Lennon's a bad
influence?" she asks.

Mom says, "John Lennon?
From the Beatles?"

The principal waves
her horrible nails.

"Lennon Wood's
a senior here,"
she says.

My heart feels dipped
in acid. Now it
crawls up my
throat like a
burning slug.

"Is that why you've been skipping?"
Mom asks.
"Is he your boyfriend?"

BOYFRIEND

Mom drives us home.
She says,
"You're not yourself lately.
What about yoga?
You haven't even
been going. I
thought you wanted to
do advanced teacher
training. Make
videos. Save up
for a studio.
What happened
to your goals?"

I shrug.

Mom says,
"Sometimes love can be toxic.
Like a drug.
It can push your
life into chaos.
Just because something
feels good,
doesn't mean it is."

I laugh till I hiccup.

HICCUP

"What's so funny?"
Mom says.

Hiccups
stab me
in between
laughs.

I choke out,
"You just described
your relationship with
Jason. You were
bored with dad.
So you found a new drug."

A NEW DRUG

When you tell the truth,
people want to
put you on meds.

Mom takes me to the
doctor. Says,
"Gabi's not herself."

The doctor listens. Then says,
"Maybe she's not supposed to be?"

For the first time,
I feel a little bit of hope.

HOPE

BANG!
BANG!
I wake up
from a dream
full of
murder.

The radiator
clangs.
Jason snores.
(Mom lets
him sleep over now.)

I cover
my ears.
But I can still
hear the radiator.
Jason. I can still
hear echoes:
Ava's voice.
Ms. Lin's
cackling laugh.
Paige's sneeze.
The gummy sound of the
rubber bands in
Kaitlyn's
braces.

I need Lennon's headphones.

HEADPHONES

Mrs. Wood's doors are locked.
But it's easy to open a window,
climb into the basement.

It's dark down here.
I shine my phone
flashlight.
Stone walls.
Dirt floor.

This place looks like
where they keep the witches
before they burn them.

I tiptoe up the stairs.
Mrs. Wood's
grandfather clock
ticks.

My breath is
tight in my
chest.

The attic feels like a long way off.

A LONG WAY OFF

I make my way
through the dark
to his bed.

I touch his shoulder.
He snorts awake.
I laugh–
and snort, too.

Lennon lifts the
covers. He says,
"Get in. It's cold."

I do.

"I'm sorry I hurt your feelings,"
he says.

His arms are warm.
So are the blankets.
I think about
Civil War moss.
It feels like the
bleeding might stop.

I sneak home at
5 a.m. Ava
texts. Even though
it's only 4 a.m. in
Iowa.

Ava: *I'm flying to Boston
Friday. There's a
shuttle service
that goes to your
town. It gets
in at six. I'll be
dropped off at the library.
Do you know where that is?*

Me: *Yes! Also.
My boyfriend
has a boat. We
can go sailing.*

Ava: *I have to
leave Monday at
nine to fly home.
Text you when
I get on the shuttle.
TTYL.*

TTYL

On Saturday
Ava posts a pic of
clam chowder.
She adds,
#Boston
#GunSenseConference
#18thbirthday.

Will it be weird
to see her? These
two months
have felt like
forever.

FOREVER

The harbor is
bright with
sails. Parents
carry coolers
to the docks.
Seagulls chase
kids, trying
to steal their
ice cream cones.
*Look at that
cute boat!*
a woman cries.
She points to the
police boat
bobbing in the harbor.

I guess that's tourism.

Jason and Mom invite
me to go on a hike.

"Let's ditch the
tourists. We can
even get away from
cell service,"
Jason says.

"I have to meet
Ava," I say.

"We'll be back by five,"
Mom says. "Doesn't
Ava get in at six?"

"I want to wait for her
here," I say.

The truth is,
Lennon hasn't
texted me back
about sailing.

But I bet
he'll be hanging
out down by the
harbor.

HARBOR

I see him
standing
far out on the
long stone jetty.
A tall dark
comma.

I walk out onto the
jetty. The wind picks
up. "Lennon!"
I call.

When he
turns, I see
Haley.

She's standing
in front of
him. Leaning
back against
his chest.

She's
so cute and
tiny–

it
would be so
easy to
push her into the
water.

123

THE WATER

"Bad news,"
Lennon says.
"My boat isn't
ready. No
sailing today."

Haley says, "Oh well. It's
freezing anyway."
She snuggles
close to him.

No, I think.
*This is
not how this
goes down.*

*Ava's coming. I
promised her we'd go
sailing with Lennon.*

*That's what I
said, and that's what
she'll get: a
boat and a
boyfriend.*

A BOAT AND A BOYFRIEND

Sure. Haley's cute.
But I know things
she doesn't.

Most people are
afraid of pain.
I'm not.
I've had so much.
I won't even
notice a little more.

Not being
afraid—
that's power.

Haley might be pretty.
But I'm
capable of anything.

CAPABLE OF ANYTHING

"So? I say. "I saw a lot of
boats around the
harbor. Why don't we just
borrow one of those?"

Lennon's eyes grow wide.
He shakes Haley off.

"Stealing a
boat is a major
crime," Haley says.

"Who does it hurt?"
I say. "We'll bring it
back. Besides.
Lots of things that
do hurt people aren't
crimes anyway."

My breath catches.
I'm thinking of
Jackson, loading
up on legal guns.

"Exactly,"
Lennon says.
"It's all a joke."

A JOKE

Haley
stalks off. Lennon
and I walk
down to the docks.

"Look for a
small boat,"
he says.
"Something
fast and easy
to sail."

The marina
is like one big
party. Every boat
plays a different
classic rock song.

Kids squeal. They
throw chips into
the water. Ducks and
gulls dive for snacks.

Then we see it.
Someone's left the
keys in a
a little red
boat with a
yellow sail.

YELLOW SAIL

I've never been
sailing before.
Lennon climbs
into the boat.
Offers me his
hand. I
step off the
dock and
into the
boat's sway.
I sit down.
The little boat
responds
to my
every move.
It's like
climbing into
a new body.
One
that can float.

FLOAT

After we leave
the harbor,
Lennon cuts the
motor.
He puts the sail up.

The boat
comes to life.

The wind fills the
yellow sail. It's like the
boat is breathing.

Each
breath
makes us
fly
forward,
cutting the
water into
white
spray.

I open my
mouth. The
wind rushes
in. I take
my first
deep
breath
in a long time.

A LONG TIME

We sail past
the island.
I look up at our
school,
perched on its
cliff.
Tiny windows flash.
I was just there
Friday. But that
seems like
a long time ago.
I promise myself:
Next time I'm in
class, I'll remember
this.

"Hold on," Lennon says.
The boat tilts.
The sail billows.
We shoot forward.
I cling onto the side of the
boat, balancing
like in a tough yoga
pose. We're
tilting so far
over my
hair
drags in the
icy water.
I think of the bird
flapping in my chest.
Now I'm flying on its
back.

Lennon guides the
boat into a quiet
cove. Dark pines
sprout from rocky
cliffs.

"Let's drop anchor.
Stay awhile,"
Lennon says.

"Okay," I say.
"We have to
get Ava at six, though."

"No problem," he says.
"We can dock
the boat at
my grandma's.
I can take her car.
We can pick
Ava up and
sneak the boat
back late
tonight."

"Okay," I say.

"For now,
let's just
float."

JUST FLOAT

There is
nothing here
but sea and
sky and
wood and
stone and
Lennon
and me.

"It's like when the
Puritans came," I say.
"Or before that.
Before guns."

"Yeah," Lennon says.
"It feels good
to get away."

AWAY

Luckily
we didn't just
steal a boat.

We also stole
snacks. There's a
cooler on board.
Diet Coke. Smoked
oysters. Trail mix.

We lie back,
snacking in the
sun, water
trickling
against the hull.

"The boat sounds
ticklish," I say,
and Lennon
grabs my foot.
But he doesn't
tickle it,
just holds on.

I breathe in
sunlight. I
feel a part of
everything, of the
wind and
water and
ancient rocks.

134

ROCKS

At first I think
the siren is
a bird.
Then Lennon
says, "Uh-oh. Cops."

I turn around.
The sailboat lurches
like it's
part of me.

I see the
police boat.
But it's not
so cute
anymore.

It's charging at us.

Can we escape?

I look around.
The cove—
the rocks and
trees—traps us.

Lennon shakes his head. Says,
"Nowhere to run.
Last kiss?"

LAST KISS

FYI:
It's not actually fun
to kiss someone,
even passionately,
when the cops are closing in.

THE COPS ARE CLOSING IN

The police boat
pulls up.
The motor
cuts out.
The siren, too.

The harbormaster
walks out on
deck. She sips a
Starbucks.

"Hi, Julie,"
Lennon says.

"Julie used to
babysit me,"
he tells me
with a grin.

The harbormaster
stirs her drink.

"Yes, Lennon. I did
babysit you.
But this isn't
just another
time-out.
This time,
you're under
arrest."

ARREST

It happens
fast. She
climbs aboard
our little
wooden boat,
handcuffs me,
and hauls
me into the
police boat.

BOAT

The boat races to
shore. Two
police cars
wait on a
lonely beach.
Their tire
tracks
snake across
the sand.

"Look,"
the harbormaster says.
"A police car
for each of you.
How cute."

CUTE

"Julie," Lennon says.
"We were just
borrowing the
boat. We can
return it.
I'll even
replace the
pretzels I
ate. I had six."

"Don't get cute,"
Julie says.

"OK." Lennon
makes his voice
serious. "My
grandma's
arthritis is so bad.
I don't want her to
come down and
pick me up.
Can the
police just
drop me at home?"

"Home?"
Julie snorts.
"Stealing a boat is
a felony.
You're not going home."

NOT GOING HOME

The town jail is in
the same big
stone
building as
the library.

Oh, no.
Ava! Her bus
drops her off
at the library.

A police
officer
presses my
finger in
ink as I
stare at
the clock
on the wall.

Ava's coming
in two hours. But
how can I
meet up with her
when I'm in jail?

JAIL

They take my
clothes. Give me scrubs
to wear. Then they
take my phone.

"We're trying to
call your mom,"
Julie says.
"But there's no
answer."

"She's hiking,"
I say. "Also.
my friend is
coming on
the shuttle.
If I don't pick her up,
she'll worry
that something
happened—"

Julie cuts me
off. "We'll
try to reach your mom."

"You can call
my dad, too."
I give her the
number.
Julie says,
"I'll do my best."

The holding cell is
a tan cube.
It's just big enough
for me.
The walls
feel rubbery.

Also:
I can hear
a woman
screaming.

Julie says,

"Don't worry
about her.
She's in withdrawal
from drugs.
She'll
scream for a
day or two."

A *day or two?*
I think. *How
long will I
be in here?*

HOW LONG WILL I BE IN HERE?

People have scratched
their names
into the wall.
Plus words
like
freedom and
justice.

I trace the letters
with my finger.
Then I find the name
Lily.

LILY

Was this
what happened
to Lennon's sister
before she died?

Did she come here
screaming?

In pain?

Clawing
her name
on the wall?

I listen to the
woman
next to me.

Red tag,
I think.
Red tag!

But no one
comes to
the rescue.

RESCUE

By now,
Ava must be
waiting
outside the
library,
wondering if I'm
dead—

My chest is
tight. My heart
feels squeezed.
I can't breathe.

It's probably just
panic, but
could I be
having a
heart
attack?
What if I am?

I stand up and
scream for help
like the woman
next door.

No one comes.

We scream and
scream together.

TOGETHER

It turns out
screaming
is just
exhaling
loudly.

When my voice
runs out,
my chest
feels
better.

My breath
feels smoother.

My body
feels
quieter.

Did I just
discover
a new
yoga move?

Am I doing
Scream
Yoga?

Jail Yoga?

JAIL YOGA

I start on
all fours.
Tabletop.
Then I flow
up into downward
dog. Back down
into plank.
Up into
cobra. The cell
fills with my
animal
shapes.

ANIMAL SHAPES

Heat
prickles on my
face. My heart
pounds. Sweat
splats on the
cell floor.
I keep moving.
Then it happens.

THEN IT HAPPENS

I'm sweating.
Balancing.
Focusing.

Suddenly a
feeling of
ease
flows into me.

My muscles
relax. I
close my
eyes. See
the boat's
yellow
sail. Feel
the warm
sun. See the
yellow
sway of the
curtains
at Bliss
Yoga.

I open my
eyes.
Blink.
See the writing
on the wall.
Freedom.

FREEDOM

Nothing's
changed.
The thought
of what
comes next–
Mom, Ava,
court, a trial–
terrifies me.

But somehow
for a minute,
I escaped
the tan cell.

I escaped
the bullets
that explode
in my mind.

I escaped–
that is, I
let my
breath escape.

I found a tiny
raft of freedom.

It feels like a promise.

PROMISE

Dad picks me up
the next
morning. He
stomps into the
jail, hollering.

At first
I think
he's mad
at me.
Then I hear
what he's saying,

"What is wrong
with you people?
Locking up a kid
overnight?
I'm her dad.
Let her out
for God's sake!"

I've never
heard him
yell.
Who knew
he could
care so much?

WHO KNEW HE COULD CARE SO MUCH?

Dad ran into
Ava at the airport.
She was getting
on her plane,
going back
home.
He was
coming here.
"Was she mad?"
I ask.

"She was...
busy," Dad says.
"Did you know
she has two
phones now?"

TWO PHONES NOW

Mom takes my phone.
I'm super grounded.

"Did you see Ava?"
 I ask.

Mom says, "Yes.
I got back
late from hiking.
Saw her
sitting on the
porch. My heart
stopped. I
thought something
happened to you.
I didn't know what
to do."

WHAT TO DO

Dad takes forever
making a
checkers move.

We're sitting
on the porch.
Lilac scent
drifts by. It
takes me back.
We could be in
Iowa. In our
old house
with the lilac
bushes.

But if we'd
stayed there,
if Mom hadn't
left Dad–
I'd be dead.

Dad jumps
my king,
says:
"Lucky me."

LUCKY ME

A police car
pulls up. My
breath catches.
Dad pats
my hand.
Julie climbs
the porch
steps, says,

"Gabi. You're
in luck. The
owner of the boat
won't press charges."

I sigh.
The wind
does, too.
The lilacs
shake with
relief.

RELIEF

Julie says,
"In fact,
the owner
changed his
story. He says
he told you to
take the boat.
Is that true?"

I swallow.

"Whose boat
was it?" Dad
asks.

"Mr. Burgos.
Gabi's teacher.
Said he didn't
realize
it was his
student who took
his boat out.
Said you had a
project.
Something to do
with Moby Dick?"

MOBY DICK

I stay after
school. Talk
to Mr. Burgos.
"I'm sorry I
stole your boat."

He says, "You sorry
about eating
my snacks too?"

"Yes," I say. "That's
why I baked you
these."

I offer him a
tray of sugar
cookies. They're
shaped like whales.
With white
frosting.

FROSTING

Mr. Burgos
crunches
a whale's head.
"I shouldn't
be eating these.
I have diabetes."
He chews.
Swallows.
Sighs.
Takes another bite.
He says,
"It's just like
in the book.
Sometimes
the white whale,
the very thing
you want most,
spells your
doom."

DOOM

"Why did you
lie to the cops
for me?" I ask.

"I didn't lie,"
he says.
"I remembered.
You have a
Moby Dick
project to do."

He opens
the book.
Turns to the
last page.

THE LAST PAGE

"'And I only am escaped alone to
tell thee,'" he reads.
"That happened
to you, too.
You survived
the shooting–
even if you weren't
there.
You lived
to tell the tale.
The world needs
to hear it."

HEAR IT

I always thought
the shooting was
Ava's story.
She lived
it. She has the
reporter voice.
A podcast. A
zillion
Twitter followers.

Mr. Burgos
nibbles a
whale's tail.

"But I don't know
what to say," I
tell him.

He smiles.
"You don't find words.
Words find you."

WORDS FIND YOU

After school,
I go to the
motel
where Dad is
staying. I
don't think.
Just open
my mouth.
The words
come.

"Why did
you just
let Mom
take me?"
I ask.
"I needed you.
Why did
you wait
until now
to come
check on me?
Sometimes it's
like you're
not even my
dad."

DAD

He turns off
the TV, says,
"You're right."

He unzips
his shaving
case. Takes
out a bottle
of pills.
Prozac.

"I've been depressed
for a long time.
Years. Your
mom wanted me
to do something
about it. I
wouldn't.
I didn't think
she would leave.
And when she
started talking
about it, I
didn't mind.
I just felt...
numb."

NUMB

"Numb," I say.
"That's how I felt.
After it happened."

I think about Lennon.
About breaking
into Captain Crab's.
Stealing the boat.
Those things
cracked the
ice around
my heart. They
made me feel
something, which is
better than
nothing.

"Numb is an awful
feeling," I say.

"I'm sorry,"
Dad says.
"I know
depression isn't an
excuse.
But it's all
I got."
He frowns.
"Are you okay?
Has it been
okay here,
with your mom?"

165

MOM

Mrs. Wood
comes to
visit. Mom
asks her in.
Pours her
coffee.
Mrs. Wood's
hands shake.
"Lennon
wanted me
to tell you
goodbye,"
she says.
"His parents
sent him
to a boarding
school. It's
a ranch.
For troubled
boys. I
don't know
when I'll
see him
again.
I haven't
been
a very
good
grandmother."

GOOD GRANDMOTHER

I hug Mrs.
Wood. "That's
not true," I
say. "Lennon
loves you
very much."

A tissue
shakes
in her hand.

"Lily
died on
my watch.
Now Lennon—
theft? This all
falls on me."

"Please,"
I beg. "This wasn't
Lennon's fault.
It was me. I wanted
to steal the boat.
I got caught
up in the moment—"

CAUGHT UP IN THE MOMENT

I don't have a phone.
But I can still check
my email at school.
Shayla
writes,
"Ava's in a
treatment center.
For exhaustion.
Which makes it
sound like she's
a movie star.
But she's
been acting
weird. Doing
way too much.
Maybe she
just needed
to fall apart."

FALL APART

I use
glue sticks and
scissors.
Make a
card
for Ava.
Everyone's
falling apart.
Dad.
Ava.
Mrs. Wood.
(She cries a lot.
Feels guilty.
Hunches over.
Gets backaches.)
Even Mr. Burgos.
(He has a new
limp.)

Hurt is all
around us.
Like water.
I want to learn to
swim.

SWIM

I climb down
Mrs. Wood's
back steps.
Wade into
the ocean.

The wind
blew Mrs. Wood's
hat off her head
and into the
sea.

I fetch
the dripping
cap. Climb back
up. The wind
whips my
wet shirt.
It sounds
like a
sail.

SAIL

Mom
lets me
help
Mrs. Wood.
Otherwise,
I'm still
grounded.
I drag a
recliner
into her
kitchen.
She puts her
feet up.
I sweep and scrub.
She teaches
me to
steam clams.

"Would you
like to go
sailing one
day?" Mrs.
Wood asks.
"They've
got my
son's boat
in the harbor now.
I can hire
a captain.
Maybe in June?"

Summer vacation
starts in
three days.
We have a
lockdown
drill all
the same.

Block the door.
Turn off the
lights. Hide.

Only, I don't.

I go the window.
Listen to the
waves. Remember
gliding by in
a boat with
yellow sails.

Someone
taps my arm.
I turn.
It's Haley, asking,
"Are you okay?"

OKAY

Haley and I
hide behind the
filing cabinets.
There's only
room for two.

She whispers,
"I'm sorry. I haven't
been very nice
to you. Lennon's
awesome. But he
didn't bring out
my best self.
He was so
hot and cold.
I never knew
where I stood.
I felt desperate,
all the time.
Jealous."

JEALOUS

"I know what you mean,"
I say. Haley
keeps talking.

"He always thought
I was shallow. A
goody-goody.
Not deep.
Then you came
along.
The Queen of Deep—"

THE QUEEN OF DEEP

The loudspeaker
crackles. The
sound brings me
back to Ava's
broadcast.
Once again
I'm in the
U-Haul,
panicked.

"I'm not the
Queen of
Deep," I tell Haley.
"Just the Queen
of deep breaths."

I breathe slowly.
Wait for the
wave of fear to
pass.

PASS

"My turn,"
I tell
Haley.
"I'm sorry too.
Look at me.
I'm a mess.
Clearly.
But Lennon
made me feel–
something.
I don't know.
Understood?
Free? Alive?
I had
to keep feeling
that way.
I didn't mean
to hurt you.
Or steal your
boyfriend. Or
whatever."

WHATEVER

On the first
day of summer
vacation, I go
to Mrs. Wood's.

Spread
my yoga
mat
in her yard.

"I found
my yoga teacher
training notes.
I think I can
help you with
your hip,"
I say.

"No," she says.
"It will hurt."

"We'll be
gentle,"
I promise.

I show her
tiny movements.
"Healing
doesn't have
to hurt,"
I say. "Even
little things
make a difference."

Shayla
writes again.
Says Ava's
coming
home in
July.
Maybe I
can plan a trip
to Iowa?

Shayla says she's
saved money
from her job
at Dairy Queen.
She can buy
half my ticket.

TICKET

When I get
to Mrs. Wood's,
I'm surprised to
see Mr. Burgos.

"Jerry's got hip
problems too,"
Mrs. Wood says.
"Will you show him
what you taught me?"

I help them
into bound
angle pose.

"Relax," I say.
"Let gravity
do the work."

Mr. Burgos
sighs, "That's
the ticket."

Mrs. Wood
says, "Can
we do this
again Friday?"

I walk into Mrs.
Wood's kitchen and see
Haley.

She's drinking
tea with
Mr. Burgos.

"Sorry,"
Haley says. "I wanted to
check on Lennon.
I don't mean
to crash your plans."

Mrs. Wood
waves her hand.
"Lennon's OK.
Kids at the
ranch aren't
allowed to communicate.
But the teachers there
say he's doing well.
The school is
is mostly
camping.
It sounds
like a lot of
pooping in the woods
to me.
Leaf toilet
paper.
But he'll live."

180

HE'LL LIVE

The words
make my
eyes sting.

Mrs. Wood says,
"Haley, would
you like to join
us for yoga?"

I look at
Haley. Tell her,
"It's not a
fast flow.
I'm not a Go Go
kind of yogi.
I'm just
trying to
help them with
some hip pain."

"That sounds
nice,"
Haley says.

We don't have
enough mats.
But the lawn
is soft.

A car
drives by.
It honks at
us. We must
look funny.

A ghost girl

a hot girl

two old people

doing
cat pose in
the grass.

When I end the
little class,
we all say
"Namaste."
*The light in me
bows to the light
in you.*

THE LIGHT

Mrs. Wood and
I go sailing.

This boat
is much
bigger
than the boat
I stole. A
captain with
a red beard
does all the
work.

Mrs. Wood and I
eat grapes and chat.
The wind blows.
The sails fill.
The boat flies
forward.

FORWARD

Mrs. Wood
talks about
her life.
She's 80
years old.
That means
she's lost
so many
people:
Her husband.
Lily.
Parents, aunts,
uncles, cousins.
Her sister. Her
best friend—

BEST FRIEND

I start to
cry. There's
so much wind.
It yanks at my
tears.
I miss
Ava. I
don't know
if we'll
ever *really*
be friends
again. Maybe our
friendship
died that
day in
March.

I look at
Mrs. Wood.
Her eyes sparkle
when she's
happy.

But the
the truth is,
death's
taken a bite
out of her.

How do
her eyes
still sparkle?

SPARKLE

"Do you
want to talk
about it?"
Mrs. Wood
says.

I stare into the
glittering
water. It's
so dark.
Yet it holds
so much
sunlight.

I open my
mouth. Let
the words
find me.

THE WORDS FIND ME

The wind quiets.
The sail goes
limp. I talk about
American history.

The wind
rises as I speak.
It fills the red sail
with air and we
fly forward,
into the sunlight.

I take attendance.
I call roll.
I say the
names.

As the names
leave my lips,
the wind lifts them up,
carries them
across the water
into the sky.

WANT TO KEEP READING?

If you liked this book, check out another book
from West 44 Books:

Tough as Lace
By Lexi Bruce

ISBN: 9781978595514

Who I Am

My name is Lacey,
but I am not
like lace.

I am bruises.
I am turf burn.
I am mud-caked cleats
and I am sweat stains.

I am lightning
on the lacrosse field.
Swerving
around defenders
and shooting
the ball past goalies.

I am not
delicate and for show.
I am not so special
that mud will ruin me.

I am not here
to look pretty
at the dining room table.

I am here to do
what I have to.

I am here to win.

Winning Together

After Friday afternoon practice,
I walk with my best friend–
and goalie–Jenna.
Head over to our favorite
hangout spot,
Rosie's Juice and Smoothie Bar.
Meet up with
my boyfriend,
Owen.

I notice him as soon
as we walk in.
He looks up
and waves at us.
Then runs
his fingers
through his messy,
dark hair.

He's sitting at a table,
sipping a mango-berry smoothie.
Reading *The Glass Menagerie*
for English on Monday.

He already ordered
my favorite smoothie for me,
mixed berry
with lots of ginger.

He closes his book
and kisses me
when I sit down
next to him.

Jenna goes up to the counter
to place her order.

"How was practice?"
Owen asks
as I take my first
sip of the smoothie.

"Really great,"
I say.
"I think
this is gonna be
my season!"

"I can't believe
I'm dating the greatest
lacrosse star
in the state,"
Owen says.

"Oh, cut it out.
You know that's
not true. I'm really only
the *second* greatest
lacrosse star
in New York,"
I joke and kiss him.

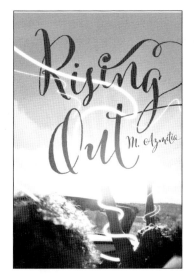

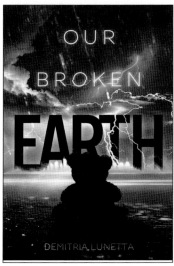

CHECK OUT MORE BOOKS AT:
www.west44books.com

An imprint of Enslow Publishing

WEST **44** BOOKS™

ABOUT THE AUTHOR

Max Howard is the author of THE WATER YEAR and FIFTEEN AND CHANGE. Max can never seem to find matching socks, but sometimes manages to find the right words.